Chapter 1
Whispers

"This is the very best day," said Amanda. "Lollipop is coming to play."

"You made up a poem!" said Mother.

"Yes, I did," said Amanda.

While she waited for Lollipop,
Amanda skipped rope.

"Today is the best day," she sang.
"Lollipop is coming to play."

But Lollipop did not come.

"Lollipop is late. I hate to wait,"
sang Amanda. "Oops, it's another
poem!"

Dear Parents and Educators,

Welcome to Penguin Young Readers! As parents and educators, you know that each child develops at his or her own pace—in terms of speech, critical thinking, and, of course, reading. Penguin Young Readers recognizes this fact. As a result, each Penguin Young Readers book is assigned a traditional easy-to-read level (1–4) as well as a Guided Reading Level (A–P). Both of these systems will help you choose the right book for your child. Please refer to the back of each book wfor specific leveling information. Penguin Young Readers features esteemed authors and illustrators, stories about favorite characters, fascinating nonfiction, and more!

| Oliver and Amanda | LEVEL 3 |
| Amanda Pig and Her Best Friend Lollipop | GUIDED READING LEVEL L |

This book is perfect for a **Transitional Reader** who:
• can read multisyllable and compound words;
• can read words with prefixes and suffixes;
• is able to identify story elements (beginning, middle, end, plot, setting, characters, problem, solution); and
• can understand different points of view.

Here are some **activities** you can do during and after reading this book:
• Problem/Solution: In each chapter of this book, there is a problem. But for each problem, there is a solution. For example, Lollipop falls, and Mother tries to make her feel better. But Lollipop won't talk. This is the problem. The solution is that Lollipop whispers to Mother where it hurts, and Mother kisses her knee to make it better. Find other problems and solutions in the book.
• Compare/Contrast: Amanda and Lollipop are best friends. Discuss how they are alike and how they are different.

Remember, sharing the love of reading with a child is the best gift you can give!

—Bonnie Bader, EdM
  Penguin Young Readers program

*Penguin Young Readers are leveled by independent reviewers applying the standards developed by Irene Fountas and Gay Su Pinnell in *Matching Books to Readers: Using Leveled Books in Guided Reading*, Heinemann, 1999.

For Elizabeth and Karen—JVL

For Ron—AS

Penguin Young Readers
Published by the Penguin Group
Penguin Group (USA) Inc., 375 Hudson Street, New York, New York 10014, USA
Penguin Group (Canada), 90 Eglinton Avenue East, Suite 700, Toronto, Ontario M4P 2Y3, Canada
(a division of Pearson Penguin Canada Inc.)
Penguin Books Ltd., 80 Strand, London WC2R 0RL, England
Penguin Group Ireland, 25 St. Stephen's Green, Dublin 2, Ireland (a division of Penguin Books Ltd.)
Penguin Group (Australia), 250 Camberwell Road, Camberwell, Victoria 3124, Australia
(a division of Pearson Australia Group Pty. Ltd.)
Penguin Books India Pvt. Ltd., 11 Community Centre, Panchsheel Park, New Delhi—110 017, India
Penguin Group (NZ), 67 Apollo Drive, Rosedale, Auckland 0632, New Zealand
(a division of Pearson New Zealand Ltd.)
Penguin Books (South Africa) (Pty.) Ltd., 24 Sturdee Avenue,
Rosebank, Johannesburg 2196, South Africa

Penguin Books Ltd., Registered Offices: 80 Strand, London WC2R 0RL, England

The full-color artwork was prepared using carbon pencil, colored pencils, and watercolor washes.
It was then color-separated and reproduced as red, blue, yellow, and black halftones.

Text copyright © 1998 by Jean Van Leeuwen. Illustrations copyright © 1998 by Ann Schweninger.
All rights reserved. First published in 1998 by Dial Books for Young Readers and in 2000 by Puffin Books,
imprints of Penguin Group (USA) Inc. Published in 2012 by Penguin Young Readers, an imprint of
Penguin Group (USA) Inc., 345 Hudson Street, New York, New York 10014. Manufactured in China.

The Library of Congress has cataloged the Dial edition under the following Control Number: 97019941

ISBN 978-0-14-037999-0   10 9 8 7 6 5 4 3

Amanda Pig
and Her Best Friend Lollipop

by Jean Van Leeuwen
pictures by Ann Schweninger

Penguin Young Readers
An Imprint of Penguin Group (USA) Inc.

Contents

Then, suddenly, there was Lollipop.

"This is my best friend Lollipop," said Amanda.

"Hello, Lollipop," said Mother. But Lollipop did not say anything.

"Let's play!" said Amanda. She showed Lollipop her room and all her toys and Sallie Rabbit.

"I have a rabbit, too," said Lollipop. "Her name is Gloria. Next time I will bring her."

Amanda and Lollipop played
School. They played Build the
Biggest City in the Whole World.

"Would you girls like a snack?"
asked Mother.

Lollipop did not say anything. But
she whispered in Amanda's ear.

"Yes!" said Amanda.

They had milk and cookies.

"Would you like another cookie?"
asked Mother.

Lollipop whispered in Amanda's
ear. "Yes, please," said Amanda.

Mother whispered in Amanda's ear.
"Why won't Lollipop talk to me?"

"She is shy," whispered Amanda.

Amanda and Lollipop played
Ballet. They did pirouettes until they
got so dizzy, they both fell down.

"I bet you girls would like a drink,"
said Mother. "Grape or apple juice?"
Lollipop whispered in Amanda's ear.
"Apple," said Amanda.

With their juice, they had lollipops.
"How did you know Lollipop loves
lollipops more than anything?"
asked Amanda.

"Oh, I just guessed," said Mother.

Amanda and Lollipop went outside.
They took turns on the swing.

"I swung so high, my toes touched the sky," said Amanda. "Hey, it's a poem again!"

"Let me try," said Lollipop. She swung so high into the sky that she fell off.

"Mother!" called Amanda.

Mother came running. She picked up Lollipop. "Where does it hurt?" she asked.

Lollipop did not say anything. She was crying.

"Here?" said Mother. She kissed Lollipop's elbow. "Here?" She kissed her ear.

Lollipop whispered in Mother's ear.

"Oh, there!" said Mother. She kissed

Lollipop's knee. "All better."

And they both smiled.

Chapter 2
The Babies

The next day Lollipop brought her
rabbit to play.

"Sallie," said Amanda, "this is
Gloria. Look, they like each other.
Maybe they will be best friends, too."

"I know what," said Lollipop. "Let's play that they are our babies."

"Good idea," said Amanda. They dressed their babies.

"It is cool today," said Lollipop. "I think they will need sweaters."

Then they fed them.

"Sallie loves bananas," said Amanda.

"So does Gloria," said Lollipop.
"But she is a little fussy today. She is
teething, you know."

Then they got the babies ready for
a walk.

"We better change their diapers
first," said Lollipop. "And put on
their hats."

"You know a lot about babies," said Amanda.

"I have a baby sister," said Lollipop. "Eat and sleep, eat and sleep. That's all they ever do."

"Sallie is awake now," said Amanda.

"Look, Sallie. See the pretty leaves."

"And the bird," said Lollipop.

"And Oliver," said Amanda.

"Do you want to play Jump in All the Leaf Piles?" asked Oliver.

Lollipop whispered in Amanda's ear.

"No," said Amanda. "We have to take care of our babies."

They walked some more. "Uh-oh,"
said Lollipop. "Gloria is crying."

"What is the matter?" asked Amanda.

"It is her teeth again," said Lollipop.
"But she likes it when I sing to her.
'Hush, little baby, don't you cry. Teeth
are good to eat with.'"

"That was almost a poem," said
Amanda.

Oliver jumped out of a leaf pile.

"Want to play Hide-and-Seek in the leaves?" he asked.

Lollipop whispered in Amanda's ear.

"One of our babies is sick," said Amanda. "Don't bother us."

"I think it is nap time," said Lollipop. They wheeled the babies home. They made a bed for them in the big chair and tucked them in, nice and cozy.

"Now do you want to play?" Oliver took a great, big jump into the big chair.

"Watch out!" cried Amanda.

"Our babies!" said Lollipop.

"You squashed them."

"Sorry," said Oliver.

Amanda and Lollipop hugged the babies.

Amanda whispered in Lollipop's ear. "You yelled at Oliver. Maybe you're not shy anymore."

"Maybe not," said Lollipop.

And they rocked their babies to sleep.

"'Rock-a-bye, babies,'" they sang,

"'in the treetops.'"

Chapter 3
Lollipop's House

Lollipop had the best house. She had a purple room.

"I love purple," said Amanda.

"I painted it all by myself," said Lollipop. "With my father."

She had bunk beds. And a whole closet full of dress-up clothes. And best of all, she had her baby sister. Lulu was her name.

"Baby sisters are much better than big brothers," said Amanda.

"Can we play with her?"

"Later," said Lollipop. "Now she has to have lunch."

Amanda and Lollipop played
games on the couch.

"Your mother lets you?" said
Amanda.

"Sure," said Lollipop.

That was another good thing
about Lollipop's house.

"Can we play with Lulu yet?" asked Amanda.

"Now she is having her nap," said Lollipop.

Amanda and Lollipop played Cooking.

"You can use real food?" said Amanda.

"Of course," said Lollipop.

That was another great thing about Lollipop's house.

They mixed up peanut butter and
marshmallows and applesauce.

"Mmm, yummy," said Amanda.

They mixed up mustard and jam
and cinnamon and pickles.

"Disgusting!" said Lollipop.

They went to the kitchen to clean
up. There was Lulu, having a snack.

"What did I tell you?" said Lollipop.
"Eat and sleep, eat and sleep."

"Is that really all she can do?"
asked Amanda.

"Well," said Lollipop, "she can play Peekaboo. And throw things. And she is learning to talk. She says 'Bye-bye' and 'Papa' and 'Mama.' But she can't say 'Lollipop.'"

"Let's teach her," said Amanda. She held up a lollipop.

"Peeky-boo," said Lulu.

"No, no," said Amanda. "Lollipop."

"Googy googy gaga," said Lulu.

"See what I mean?" said Lollipop.

She took a lick of her lollipop.

"Look, Lulu," she said. "Lolly. Pop."

"Oopy doop," said Lulu.

"I give up," said Lollipop.

It was time to go home. "Don't worry," said Amanda. "Next time I come to play, we will give her another lesson. Good-bye, everyone."

"Bye, Amanda," said Lollipop.

"Come again," said Lollipop's mother.

"Mamba," said Lulu.

"Did you hear that?" said Amanda. "She said my name!"

"Bye-bye, Mamba," said Lulu.

And that was the very best thing about Lollipop's house.

Chapter 4
The Sleepover

Amanda loved Lollipop's house. She loved it so much, she wished she didn't have to go home.

"I know what!" said Lollipop. "Tomorrow you can sleep over."

"Can I? Can I? Can I?" begged
Amanda.

"Are you sure you want to?"
said Father.

"Yes, yes, yes, yes, yes!" said Amanda.

So she packed her little suitcase and
went to sleep at Lollipop's house. She
and Lollipop played with Lulu.

They played Peekaboo and Pick Up Lulu's Toys.

"Say 'Lollipop,'" said Amanda.

"Lollipop, Lollipop, LOLLIPOP!"

"Olli-op," said Lulu at last.

"She did it!" said Lollipop. "Hooray!"

They had popcorn and root-beer floats. Lollipop's house had super snacks.

Then it was time for bed.

"Do you want the top bunk or the bottom?" asked Lollipop.

"The top," said Amanda. "It's like sleeping in a tree."

Lollipop's mother tucked them in.

"Now," said Lollipop, "we can talk all night."

They played What Is Your Favorite? "What is your favorite ice cream?" asked Lollipop.

"Strawberry," said Amanda. "What is your favorite color?"

Lollipop did not say anything.

"Lollipop?" said Amanda. "I can't believe it. She is asleep."

Amanda tried to go to sleep. But her eyes kept popping open. It felt strange to be up so high. If she moved, she might fall out.

And what were all those funny
shadows? Maybe one of them was
a monster.

Squeak! went something at the window.
"What was that?" whispered Amanda.

Squeak! Tap, tap, tap!

A monster's claws were scratching at the glass. Amanda hid way down under the covers. She hugged Sallie Rabbit tight.

"What is the matter," she said, "that makes your teeth chatter? That was a scary poem."

She wished Oliver was there. He
would say, "Don't be dumb. There is
no such thing as monsters."

Father would chase the monster
away. "I want to go home,"
whispered Amanda.

She waited until the monster was quiet. Then very carefully she climbed down and tiptoed out of Lollipop's room.

The house was dark. Everything was still. Amanda found the telephone.

"Hello," said Father's sleepy voice.

"I changed my mind," said
Amanda. "I don't want to sleep over."

"But I am asleep," said Father.
"And it is raining outside."

"Please?" said Amanda.

"I will be right there," said Father.

They walked home in the rain.

"The bed was too high," said

Amanda. "And it was too dark. And

there was a monster at the window."

"It was only the rain," said Father.

"Maybe," said Amanda. "But you know what? I like Lollipop's house in the daytime. But at night I like my own house."